# Lily Lemon Blossom

## Where is Lily's Miss Kelly Kay?

Story by Barbara Miller
Illustrations by Inga Shalvashvili

Lily has a lovely doll
she calls Miss Kelly Kay.
She was a gift from her mother
on her third birthday.

She has big brown eyes,
long black hair and
poor Lily cannot
find her anywhere.

She is not under the bed
with bunny and bear.

She is not behind the pillows
on the pink polka dot chair.

She is not hiding
in kangaroos pouch.

She is not sleeping with Josephine
and Mia the mouse.

Maybe thought Lily, she is in
the garden on the swing...

or playing under the tree
with her friend Evergreen.

But alas, there was no Miss Kelly Kay.
Lily looked everywhere
Miss Kelly Kay would play.

As Lily stopped to think
what next must she do,
she heard someone say,
"hi Lily, we have a surprise for you."

It was her friends
Jasmine and Jamie,
the Paisley twins.

"We found our missing dolls, Happy Face, Dots and your Miss Kelly Kay. Sugar Pie hid them in her doggie house today."

"They were all napping in Sugar Pie's bed. We hurried to bring her home to you," Jamie said.

"Oh my lovely Miss Kelly Kay.
I thought I'd lost you,
don't ever go away.
Thank you Jasmine and
Jamie for bringing her
home to me. We must
celebrate. I know, cookies
and tea!"

"Miss Kelly Kay come sit with bunny and bear. Your old and new friends would like you to share, the fun time you had with Happy Face and Dots, while we set the table with my cups and teapot."

Lily and her friends laughed, talked and sipped their tea. They were so happy to have solved the big mystery.

The dolls all gathered on the pink polka dot chair. Miss Kelly Kay had so much to share. She told them all about her very special day, as Lily and her friends stacked and cleared the dishes away.

Sugar pie and Josephine were having fun, playing on the window sill in the warm cosy sun. Every time Sugar Pie's tail wagged and wiggled, Josephine would grab it and make her giggle.

It turned out to be
a very good day,
for Lily, her friends
and Miss Kelly Kay.

The End

# Lily Lemon Blossom

## Children's Picture Books
## Collect Them All

Visit Lily at:

# www.lilylemonblossom.com